A Voyage in Everyday Words :

SHOPPING AND ENTERTAINMENT

Jeremy and Sara Walenn

A Voyage in Everyday Words

讓孩子走進生活，
用眼睛、耳朵及聯想力學習英語生活詞彙

你有否發現孩子在英語造句或作文時，連很常見的事物的意思也不懂表達呢？若是如此，你應該意識到，孩子迫切需要擴展生活詞彙量，提升最基本的英語溝通能力了。但是，孩子應該學些甚麼詞彙？要學多少詞彙？怎樣學才是有效的方法呢？

語言是重要的溝通工具，因此，學語言也不應該脫離生活的環境。對孩子而言，學習日常碰到及熟悉的事物的詞彙，除了有助他們理解和記憶之外，還能引發他們學習的興趣。而孩子學好了生活詞彙，他們的英語溝通能力便能大大提升！

A Voyage in Everyday Words 系列，是以嶄新的方法幫助孩子輕鬆學習英語生活詞彙的套裝。每套書由 "詞彙學習書" 及 "發音光碟" 組合而成，圍繞Cooking (煮食)、Nature (自然)、Home and Friends (家庭和朋友)、Sports and Games (運動和遊戲)、Festival (節慶) 及 Shopping and Entertainment (購物和娛樂) 六大生活主題，教導孩子 3000 個在日常生活中會碰到的常用詞彙。作者 Jeremy and Sara Walenn 具有30年教授以英語作為第二語言的人士的經驗，他們在本套裝中特別為華人小孩子挑選了最應該學懂的生活詞彙。因此，你的孩子將能熟悉西方的生活情景，又能學習到最地道的英語！

在生活情景中學習常見事物的名稱

翻閱本書，孩子將會看到一個個與主題相關的生活情景，並從中學習常見事物的名稱、詞彙和詞組。孩子可以輕輕鬆鬆學會最該學懂的生活詞彙。

利用詞彙地圖（Word Map）的概念，用聯想力學習新詞彙

除了主題詞彙，本書亦延伸選取了更多相關詞彙，着重從"詞的相近組合"及"詞的相關主題"兩大方面，幫助孩子以聯想力學習更多新詞彙。本書以有趣的詞彙地圖編排，表示詞彙的延伸關係，並配以色彩繽紛的插圖，能夠有效激起孩子學習的興趣。

讓孩子邊聽邊學標準的英語發音

書內所有詞彙和例句，都是由作者親自錄音。作者標準的英語發音，將有助於改善孩子的英語發音。左頁下方的曲目編號，對應光碟音檔的首兩個號碼，方便查找之餘，也方便選聽個別生字。

家長不妨與孩子一起翻閱本書，透過角色扮演，以生動活潑的方式學習詞彙。家長還可以與孩子一同聯想出更多的詞彙，繼續擴展孩子的詞彙量呢！

JEREMY WALENN

Jeremy Walenn graduated in Law then taught in primary schools for five years before becoming a teacher of English as a Foreign Language. He was a Director of Studies in the UK and Head of Languages at a UK university. He has been a senior examiner for international examination boards and examined in the Far East, Europe and South America. He is now working for a UK ELT publisher.

He has written EFL text books, including academic, examination and young learners' material. He is the author of *Passport to the Cambridge Proficiency Examination* (Macmillan) and the *Talking Trinity* series.

SARA WALENN

Sara Walenn began teaching English as a Foreign Language (EFL) in 1978. She is a teacher trainer, EFL author and examiner. She was a Director of Studies in the UK and is now working for a UK EFL publisher in Asia.

韋倫先生

韋倫先生擁有超過30年教導以英語作為第二語言的人士學習英語的經驗，曾於英國擔任教務長，任大學的語言中心主管。韋倫先生除了擁有豐富的教學經驗外，也是歐美及遠東多個國際考試評核局的資深考官，現為英國的出版社撰寫ELT書籍。

韋倫先生曾撰寫一系列有關準備英語國際考試的出版物，當中包括 *Passport to the Cambridge Proficiency Examination* (Macmillan) 及 the *Talking Trinity* series (Garnet publications) 等。

韋倫女士

韋倫女士自1978年開始教授以英語作為外語 (English as a Foreign Language) 的課程，了解非以英語作為母語的人士學習英語的需要。在教學之餘，她致力於培訓英語教師，並擔任EFL課程的作者和考官。韋倫女士現時於英國擔任教務長並為英國的出版社撰寫ELT書籍。

The Voyage Route 漫遊路徑

A Voyage in Everyday Words: SHOPPING AND ENTERTAINMENT

Word Map 詞彙地圖

Shopping P 10-11

Eating out P 62-63

Extra Words 焦點選字

P12-31

market, shopping arcade, hand cream,
shoes, box, wrapping paper,
note, credit card, small change,
sales assistant

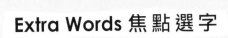

Diary

Entertainment P36-37

Extra Words 焦點選字

P38-57

ride, ticket, full house,
play, show, spotlight,
stage, film star,
screen, seat

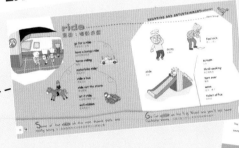

Diary

P64-83

salad dressing, salt and pepper,
birthday cake, bottle,
dish, drink, fresh food,
cook, service, tip

Extra Words 焦點選字

Diary

Chapter One

Shopping

chain store
連鎖商店

corner shop
街角小店

Internet
互聯網

market (P12)
市場

superstore
大型超級市場

shopping arcade (P14)
購物商場

places
場所

Shopping
購物

types of goods
商品的種類

comic
漫畫

digital camera
數碼相機

hand cream (P16)
潤手霜

mobile phone
行動電話

shower gel
淋浴時用的皂液

shoes (P18)
鞋子

stickers
貼紙

payment
付款

note (P24)
鈔票

cheque
支票

credit card (P26)
信用卡

coins
硬幣；錢幣

exchange (of goods)
更換

small change (P28)
零錢；找頭

store card
在特定商店使用的簽賬咭

Word Map

packaging
包裝

box (P20)
盒；箱

carrier bag
購物袋

gift box
禮盒

cling film
保鮮紙

ribbon
絲帶

foil
箔紙

wrapping paper (P22)
(禮品) 包裝紙

people
人物

cashier
收銀員；收銀處

manager
經理

sales assistant (P30)
售貨員；店員

shelf filler
理貨員

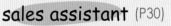

market
市場

antiques market
古玩市場

flea market
廉價市場；跳蚤市場

flower market
花市

hypermarket
大型超級市場

supermarket
超級市場

be on the market
出售

market trader
商人

market leader
市場領袖（指銷量最好的產品或它的生產廠商）

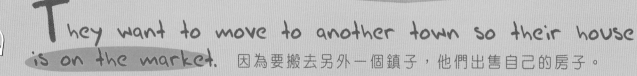

They want to move to another town so their house is on the market. 因為要搬去另外一個鎮子，他們出售自己的房子。

barrow
流動售貨車

greengrocer
菜販

home-made
自製的；家裏做的

barter
討價還價；以物易物

clear up
清理

fresh
新鮮的

set up a stall
搭建貨架

a trade/to trade
交易／做交易

I love looking around the flea market to see if I can find a bargain! 我很喜歡逛廉價市場，看看能不能找到一些便宜貨。

13

shopping arcade
購物商場

shopping bag
購物袋

shopping trip
以購物為主的旅行團

shop around
購物前逐店比較選購

shop-soiled
因有瑕疵而特價發售的（貨品）

do the weekly **shop**
每週一次的購物

amusement **arcade**
電玩遊樂場

video **arcade**
電玩遊樂場

arcade games
（遊樂場的）電玩遊戲

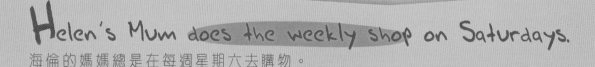

Helen's Mum does the weekly shop on Saturdays.
海倫的媽媽總是在每週星期六去購物。

Word Group

aisle
通道；走廊

information counter
查詢櫃台

concourse
廣場；（車站、機場）中央大堂

covered
有屋頂的

exclusive
獨家售賣的

expensive
昂貴的

queue
排隊

row
列；排

We went on a  last week and got lots of bargains.　上星期我們去旅行購物，買了很多便宜貨。

hand cream
潤手霜

handbag
（女士用）手提包

have your **hands** full
非常忙碌

left-**hand** drive
左座駕駛

minute **hand** (on a watch)
分針

cream
奶油；奶油色的

cream cracker
奶油蘇打餅乾

salad **cream**
一種放在沙拉上面的蛋黃醬

sour cream
酸奶油

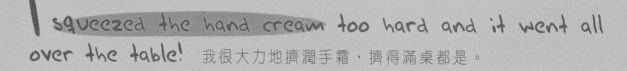

I squeezed the hand cream too hard and it went all over the table! 我很大力地擠潤手霜，擠得滿桌都是。

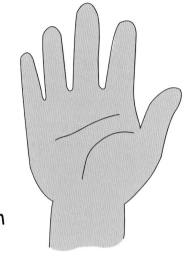

palm
手掌

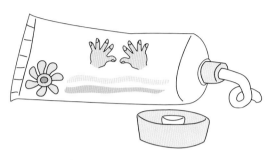

tube of hand cream
一管潤手霜

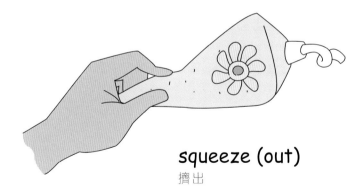

squeeze (out)
擠出

fingers
手指

moist
濕潤的

nails
指甲

scented
有香味的

apply (hand cream)
塗（潤手霜）

Would you like some salad cream on your salad?
你想加點沙拉醬在青菜沙拉上嗎？

shoes
鞋子

ballet shoes
芭蕾舞鞋

flat shoes
平底鞋

high-heeled shoes
高跟鞋

horseshoe
馬蹄鐵

running shoes
跑鞋

tennis shoes
網球鞋

shoelace
鞋帶

shoe shop
鞋店

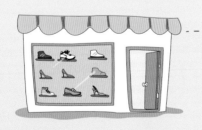

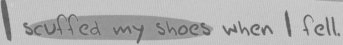

I scuffed my shoes when I fell.
我跌倒時把鞋子磨損了。

polish (your shoes)
擦鞋

flip-flops
人字拖鞋

boots
靴子

football boots
足球鞋

sandals
涼鞋

slippers
拖鞋

trainers
運動鞋

scuff (your shoes)
磨損（鞋子）

I wear my flip-flops all the time in the summer.
夏天的時候我總是穿人字拖。

19

box

盒：箱

jewellery box
首飾盒

matchbox
火柴盒

musical box
音樂盒

nesting box
鳥巢

penalty box
（足球）罰球區；（曲棍球）受罰席

shoe box
鞋盒

telephone box
公用電話亭

window box
窗台上的花盆箱

This musical box plays a lovely tune.
這個音樂盒的樂曲很動聽。

carton
硬紙盒；紙箱

pack
包裝

casket
首飾盒

paper
紙

rectangular
長方形的

square
正方形

trunk
大行李箱；（汽車的）行李箱

a safe
保險箱

The player committed a foul in the penalty box.
這個球員在罰球區內犯規。

wrapping paper
（禮品）包裝紙

wrap up a present
包裝禮物

wrap up on a cold day
在冷天穿得暖和

wrap up (a meeting/lesson/
concert)
結束（會議／課堂／音樂會）

bubble **wrap**
（用來保護物件的）氣泡膠墊

paper thin
如紙一般薄的

examination **paper**
試卷

tissue **paper**
衛生紙

writing **paper**
信紙；寫字紙

We had to wrap up well because it was such a cold day.　天氣很冷，我們要穿得暖和一些。

cover
蓋上

a fold/to fold
褶 / 摺疊

a cut/to cut
切；割；剪

pattern
花樣；圖案

present
禮物

ribbon
絲帶

sheet
一片；一張

a roll/to roll
一捲 / 捲起

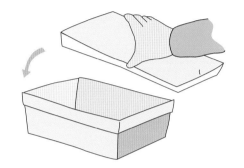

I chose a sheet of blue wrapping paper with matching ribbon for my friend's birthday present.
我選了一張藍色的包裝紙和相配的絲帶，用來包裝送給朋友的生日禮物。

note
鈔票

banknote
鈔票

musical note
音符

noted
著名的

notebook
筆記本

notebook (computer)
筆記型電腦

notepaper
便條紙；信紙

make a **note** (of something)
記錄

take **notes** (in a lesson)
（在課堂上）寫筆記

I scribbled a note for Daniel to tell him what time I was coming home. 我匆匆寫了一張便條給丹尼，告訴他我幾時回家。

spell
拼寫

a scribble/to scribble
潦草的字 / 潦草地寫

leave (a note for someone)
留（便條給某人）

read
看

rub out
擦掉

scrap of paper
一小片紙

write
寫

tear off (a piece of paper)
撕掉（一張紙）

He made a note of the nearest bus-stop to his new school so he wouldn't be late. 他記下離學校最近的巴士站，避免遲到。

credit card...
信用卡

credit (a unit of study at university)
（大學）學分

the credits
電影或電視的演員名單

be a **credit** to (someone)
給（某人）增光

(take) the **credit** (for something)
（因某事獲得）稱讚；認可

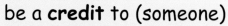

cardboard
厚紙板

greetings **card**
賀卡

playing **cards**
玩紙牌

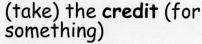

yellow **card**
（足球比賽中因犯規而得到的）黃牌

You've done so well—you're a credit to your family!
做得好，你真為你的家增光！

accept
接受

swipe
刷卡

interest charge
利息費用

××××...... $30000
interest
charge $200

apply for
申請

charge
費用

cut up
剪碎（信用卡）

rectangular
長方形的

reject
拒絕

I like playing card games with my sister.
我很喜歡和妹妹玩紙牌。

small change

零錢；找頭

small ad
（報紙上的）小廣告

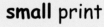

small fortune
很多錢

small hours
凌晨；深夜

small print
（合約中用小字印刷的）附屬細則

change for the better
好轉

change hands
轉手

change your mind
改變主意

climate change
氣候變化（指全球暖化的現象）

Let's toss a coin to see who starts the game!
Heads or tails? 我們擲幣來決定誰先玩吧。你猜正面還是反面？

heads (side of a coin)
（硬幣的）正面

toss a coin
擲幣

coins
硬幣

drinks machine
自動販賣飲料機

tails (the other side of the coin)
（硬幣的）反面

jangle
（硬幣等金屬互相撞擊發出的）叮噹聲

value
面值

heavy
重的

I am tired because I was up until the small hours revising for an exam. 為了考試，我溫習到深夜，所以現在覺得很累。

sales assistant
售貨員；店員

sale price
特價

sales rep
銷售代表；推銷員

charity **sale**
義賣

closing-down **sale**
清倉拍賣

summer **sales**
夏季促銷

office **assistant**
辦公室助理

personal digital **assistant** (PDA)
電子手帳

assistant editor
助理編輯

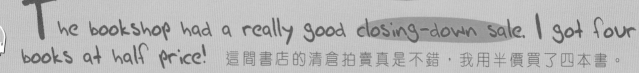

The bookshop had a really good closing-down sale. I got four books at half price! 這間書店的清倉拍賣真是不錯，我用半價買了四本書。

Word Group

show
陳列；展出

give change
找零錢

advise
建議

sell
銷售

serve
服務；侍候

special offer
特別優惠

wrap
包裝

help
幫助

The sales assistant said it was a special offer and gave us a 50% discount. 售貨員說這是特別優惠，給我們半價折扣。

Mum and I went by bus to the big **superstore** in the city centre to do the **weekly shop**. Mum wanted to buy the groceries so I sneaked off to look for a **birthday present** for my friend. I found a really nice **jewellery box**. I also got her a birthday card, some silver *wrapping paper* and different coloured ribbons. Mum told me to take the box to customer services and get it gift wrapped. I met her at the till and she paid for everything with her *credit card.*  When she saw the receipt she said the **shopping** had cost her a **small fortune!**

I went out with my friends to a really cool **shopping arcade**. It's got lots of small **shops** selling great clothes, jewellery, boots, *shoes* and cosmetics. We tried on some perfume and nail polish. I wanted to smell some *hand cream* so I **squeezed** a bit onto my **palm**. It smelt yukky! One of the **shoe shops** was having a **closing-down sale**. We had fun putting on boots and **trainers**. I really liked the pair with **high heels** and I asked the sales **assistant** to check the **sale price**. They were less than half price. A real **bargain**!

Chapter Two

Entertainment

theme parks
主題樂園

aquarium 水族館	**ride** (P38) 乘車；機動遊戲
cable car 纜車	**roller coaster** (遊樂場的) 過山車
queue 排隊	**ticket** (P40) 門票；入場券

zoo
動物園

Entertainment
娛樂

at the theatre
在劇院

actor 演員	
curtain (舞台) 幕布	
full house (P42) 滿座	**show** (P46) 展覽；表演
play (P44) 表演；戲劇；玩耍	**spotlight** (P48) 聚光燈；受公眾矚目
programme 節目	**stage** (P50) 舞台

13

Word Map

at the cinema
在電影院

action film
動作電影

advertisements
廣告

adventure films
歷險電影

film star (P52)
電影明星

front row
前排（座位）

popcorn
爆米花

screen (P54)
銀幕；屏幕

torch
手電筒

at the stadium
在運動場

cheer leaders
啦啦隊長

commentator
現場解說員；評論家

crowd
人群

marching band
步操樂隊；軍樂隊

scoreboard
積分板

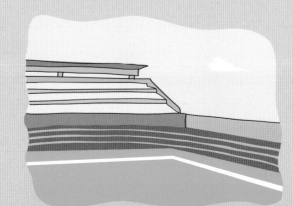

seats (P56)
座位

spectators
觀眾

wide-screen TV
闊屏幕電視

ride

乘車：機動遊戲

go for a ride
乘車旅行；兜風

have a bumpy ride
非常困難的時候

horse riding
騎馬

motorbike rider
摩托車手

ride a bus
搭乘巴士

ride out the storm
渡過難關

let it ride
任由情況繼續下去

well-ridden
騎術高超的

Some of the rides at the new theme park are really scary. 新主題樂園裏有部份機動遊戲真令人膽顫心驚。

dizzy
眩暈的

feel sick
噁心；想吐

slide
滑梯

scream
尖叫

thrill-seeking
敢於冒險的

turn over
翻倒

wave
起伏；揮手

ticket office
售票處

Go for a ride on the Big Wheel and you'll see some fantastic views. 在摩天輪上你可以觀賞到很美麗的風景。

ticket

門票：入場券

e-ticket/electronic ticket
電子票

parking/speeding ticket
違規停車 / 超速罰單

return ticket
來回票

single ticket
單程票

ticket collector
收票員

ticket machine
售票機

ticket office
售票處

15

Tickets for the World Cup final are really expensive.
世界盃決賽的門票真是太貴了。

boarding pass
登機證

tag
牌子；標籤

label
標籤；標記

No Entry (without a ticket)
無票不得入場

online booking
網上預訂

passport
護照；通行證

pay a fine (if you don't have a ticket)
（因無票入場的）罰款

travel card
旅行卡；觀光卡

James left his car on a double yellow line and got a parking ticket. 詹姆斯把車子停在雙黃線上，結果吃了一張違規停車罰單。

full house
滿座

full-grown
發育完全的；成熟的

full marks
滿分

full speed
全速（前進）

full time
全職

doll's house
玩具屋

mouse-to-house
網上購物

tree house
樹屋

Wendy house
溫蒂屋（給小孩子入內玩的玩具屋）

It's a full house tonight. There are no more tickets available.　今晚滿座，沒有多餘的門票了。

crowded
擁擠的

shuffle/deal
洗 / 發紙牌

card game
紙牌遊戲

audience
觀眾

busy
忙碌的

popular
流行的

spectators
（看比賽的）觀眾

tickets
門票；入場券

My dog is now fully-grown.
我的小狗已經長大了。

play

表演；戲劇；玩耍

fair play
公平競爭

play up
搗蛋

player
參加遊戲或比賽的人

playful
有趣的；開玩笑的

playground
（學校的）操場；遊樂場

playgroup
幼兒遊戲組

playmate
玩伴

playtime
（學校）遊戲時間；上演時間

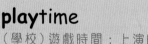

🎧 17

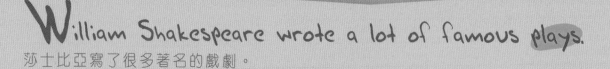

William Shakespeare wrote a lot of famous plays.
莎士比亞寫了很多著名的戲劇。

naughty
調皮的

game
遊戲

laughter
笑聲

amuse yourself
自娛

mess around
胡鬧;消磨時光

have fun
玩得開心

production
製作

recreation
消遣;娛樂

The teacher got angry when the children started to play up.

孩子開始搗蛋的時候,老師很生氣。

show
展覽；表演

chat show
聊天秀

fashion show
時裝表演

quiz show
問答比賽節目

puppet show
木偶表演

TV game show
電視遊戲節目

show business
演藝事業

show of hands
舉手表決

show off
賣弄；炫耀

Show business can be so competitive.
演藝界的競爭可以是非常激烈的。

Word Group

illustrate
舉例說明；用圖說明

presenter
（電視節目）主持人

artist
藝術家

**classroom/teacher/
students**
教室；老師；學生

demonstrate
示範

model
模特兒；榜樣；模型

host
（電視節目）主持人；主人

perform
表演

I love quiz shows because I always try to answer the questions.

我很喜歡那些問答比賽節目，因為我很喜歡試答那些問題。

spotlight...

聚光燈：受公眾矚目

beauty spot
名勝；景點

penalty spot
（曲棍球）罰球點

perfect spot
最佳位置

soft spot
偏愛（特別對於別人不喜歡的人或物）

fairy light
（用來裝飾用的）彩燈

headlight
車前大燈；（礦工，醫生等用的）頭燈

lighthouse
燈塔

overhead light
吊燈

Helen's granddad has a soft spot for her: he's always buying her presents. 海倫的祖父很偏愛她，總是給她買禮物。

19

celebrities
名人

bulb
燈泡

attention
注意力

beam
光線

famous
著名的

lamp
燈

ray
光線；視線

shadow
影子；陰暗處

Some film stars don't like being in the spotlight.
一些電影明星並不喜歡老是受大眾矚目。

stage

舞台

back stage
後台

front stage
舞台；表演區

off-stage
後台的

on stage
在舞台上

stage door
（供演員及工作人員出入的）劇場後門

stage fright
怯場

stage lighting
舞台燈光

stage manager
舞台監督

The actors bowed as the audience clapped.
這些演員鞠躬向鼓掌的觀眾致意。

clap
鼓掌

bow
鞠躬

props
小道具

arch
拱門

audience
觀眾；聽眾

curtain
幕布；窗簾

line
台詞

orchestra
管弦樂隊

Some of the children got stage fright before their performance. 有些小朋友在表演之前怯場。

film star...
電影明星

film director
電影導演

filmgoer
常去看電影的人

cartoon **film**
卡通電影

horror **film**
恐怖電影

shooting **star**
流星

star sign
星座

all-**star** cast
全明星陣容

five-**star** hotel
五星級的（第一流的）酒店

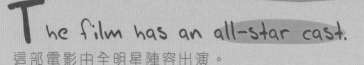

The film has an all-star cast.
這部電影由全明星陣容出演。

poster
海報

make-up
化妝；化妝品

actor/actress
男 / 女演員

beautiful
漂亮的

handsome
（男子）英俊的；（女子）迷人的；
健美的

Oscar
奧斯卡金像獎（國際電影獎項）

performer
表演者

photographer
攝影師

I like reading magazines which have stories about famous film stars. 我很喜歡看那些報導著名影星故事的雜誌。

screen

銀幕；屏幕

screen (a candidate)
篩選；遴選（候選人）

screen (a film)
拍攝

screen your eyes from the sun
保護眼睛不受陽光直接照射

screen saver
屏幕保護程式

computer **screen**
電腦顯示器

the silver **screen**
電影業

the small **screen**
電視

television **screen**
電視屏幕

The nurse pulled the curtain around the bed to screen off the patient. 護士在床的四周圍上幕布，把病人和外界隔開。

Word Group

display
陳列；表演

hide
隱藏

switch on
開啟（電器）

check
檢查

monitor
（電腦）顯示器

separate
分開

surface
表面

watch TV
看電視

There are six films showing at the multi-screen cinema.
多屏幕影院現正放映六部電影。

seat
座位

aisle seat
近走道的座位

booster seat
（汽車的）幼兒座椅

ejector seat
（飛機的）彈射座椅

passenger seat
客座

window seat
靠窗的座位

reserve a seat
預留座位

in the hot seat
困境（需要做出惹怒別人的決定）

seat belt
安全帶

50,000-seat stadium
有 50,000 個座位的體育館

You'll need to book early to get a good seat.
你要早點訂位，才能訂到好位置。

seating plan
座位圖

bench
長椅

chair
椅子

sofa
沙發

deck chair
躺椅

furniture
家具

safety belt
安全帶

sitting room
起居室；客廳

Please fasten your seat belts before take-off.
飛機起飛前，請大家繫好安全帶。

My birthday! I got a real surprise. My grandparents had bought

tickets  for a day at the theme park.

Fantastic! We got to the turnstiles just

as they were opening. I was feeling really excited.

We went to the big roller coaster first. There wasn't a queue and as

soon as we sat down the ride started. The car climbed slowly to the top

and then dropped suddenly. I screamed. On the way back it turned over

completely. I was upside down and feeling sick and *dizzy*.

I was very happy when we finally got off. It was a scary ride

but absolutely brilliant.

My parents took me to the *cinema*. We got **seats** in the middle **row** and they bought me a big tub of **popcorn**. It was dark inside so the usher showed us to our **seats** with a **torch**. There were loads of **advertisements** first and then a trailer for a **cartoon**. It looked really good. My Mum and Dad told me the main **film** was a comedy with an all-star **cast**. A comedy with an all-star **cast**?? I didn't laugh at all. I thought it was a **horror film** because it was so bad. The **actors** were really boring. I didn't recognise any of them and the soundtrack only had the sort of music old people like.

Chapter Three

Eating out

tasting and seasoning
味道和調味

bitter
苦的

salad dressing (P64)
沙律調味醬

delicious
美味的

salt and pepper (P66)
鹽和胡椒粉

sour
酸的

sweet
甜的

tasteless
沒有味道的

yukky
難吃的；難以下咽的

Eating out
上館子吃飯

choosing and booking
選擇和預約

by the window
靠窗(的位置)

fast food restaurant
快餐店

non-smoking environment
無煙環境

make a reservation
預約

time
時間

choosing and
ordering food
選擇和點菜

birthday cake (P68)
生日蛋糕

bottle (P70)
酒；瓶子

dessert
甜點

dish (P72)
菜餚；碟子

drink (P74)
飲料；喝

fresh food (P76)
新鮮的食物

main course
主菜

starter
第一道菜；開胃菜

Word Map

cooking and serving
烹調和上菜

chef
(酒店；餐廳)大廚

chef's hat
廚師帽

cook (P78)
廚師；烹調

customer
顧客

front-of-house
接待員

kitchen staff
廚房員工

service (P80)
服務；招待

tip (P82)
小費；提示

waiter/waitress
男 / 女侍應生

salad dressing
沙拉調味醬

salad bar
沙拉吧台（專門擺放各種沙拉的吧台）

salad cream
一種放在沙拉上面的蛋黃醬

fruit **salad**
水果沙拉

green **salad**
蔬菜沙拉

potato **salad**
土豆沙拉

dressing gown
浴袍；晨衣

dressing up
穿上盛裝；裝扮

window **dressing**
裝飾（商店）櫥窗

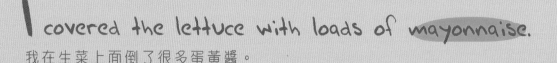

I covered the lettuce with loads of mayonnaise.
我在生菜上面倒了很多蛋黃醬。

ketchup
番茄醬

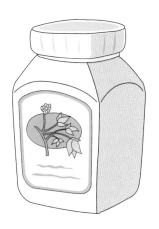

herbs
藥草；香草（可用於烹調）

stir
攪拌

keep cool
（沙拉）保持冰涼；保持鎮定

mayonnaise
蛋黃醬

mustard
芥末

oil
油

thousand island dressing
千島醬

I had a shower and then put on my dressing gown.
我先洗了澡，再穿上浴袍。

salt and pepper--
鹽和胡椒粉

a pinch of salt
一撮鹽

salt cellar
鹽瓶；鹽皿

salt water
海水；鹽水

salted peanuts
淮鹽花生

salty crisps
鹽味薯片

pepper mill
胡椒研磨器

pepper pot
胡椒瓶

sweet **pepper**
燈籠椒

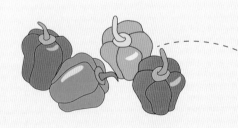

Can you grind up the peppercorns in the pepper mill?
你能用胡椒研磨器把這些胡椒子磨碎嗎？

dining table
餐桌

add
增加

grind
磨碎

herbs and spices
香草與香料

preserve (food in salt)
（用鹽）醃製（食物）

season
調味

tasteless
沒有味道的

thirsty
口渴

I always feel thirsty when I eat salted peanuts.
吃了淮鹽花生，我總會覺得很口渴。

birthday cake
生日蛋糕

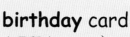

birthday card
生日賀卡

birthday party
生日派對

birthday present
生日禮物

tenth **birthday**
十歲生日

fairy **cake**
精緻的小蛋糕

pancake
烤薄餅

piece of **cake**
一塊蛋糕；很簡單的事情

sponge **cake**
海綿蛋糕；鬆糕

Helen's mum decorated her birthday cake with her favourite cartoon characters. 海倫的媽媽用海倫最喜歡的卡通人物裝飾生日蛋糕。

slice
切成薄片

bakery
麵包店

layer
層

cream
奶油

flour
麵粉

fruit tarts
水果餡餅

handmade
手工的

snack
點心；小吃

You can make a sponge cake with flour, eggs and sugar.
你可以用糖，雞蛋和麵粉作海綿蛋糕。

bottle

酒：瓶子

bottle bank
玻璃瓶回收箱

bottle green
深綠色的

bottle opener
開瓶器

bottle top
瓶蓋

bottled juice
瓶裝果汁

bottle-feed
用奶瓶餵養（嬰兒）

hot-water **bottle**
熱水袋；湯壺

water **bottle**
水壺

29

Daniel took the empty bottles to the bottle bank.
丹尼把所有空瓶子都送去回收箱了。

pour
倒出

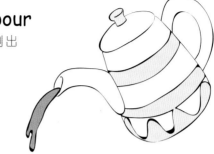

container
容器

empty
空的

full
滿的

glass
玻璃杯

plastic
塑膠的；（貶義）不自然的

volume
容積；體積

tin
罐頭；錫製的

I always take a water bottle when I go hiking.
遠足的時候我總會帶個水壺。

dish

菜餚；碟子

dish of the day
是日推介

dish rack
碟架

dish up food
把食物盛到碟子裏

do the **dishes**
洗碟子

oven-proof **dish**
耐熱碟子（烤箱適用的）

satellite **dish**
衛星電視碟形天線

spicy **dish**
味道辛辣的菜式

vegetarian **dish**
素菜；齋菜

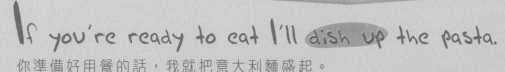

If you're ready to eat I'll dish up the pasta.
你準備好用餐的話，我就把意大利麵盛起。

cup and saucer
茶杯和碟子

ladle
勺子；長柄勺

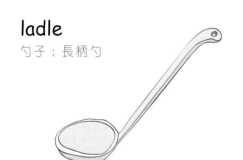

bowl
碗

container
容器（如箱、盒、罐等）

plate
碟子

serving spoon
公用勺子

signal (TV and radio)
信號

washing-up liquid
洗潔精

Our satellite dish can receive TV signals from all over the world. 我們的天線能接收全世界的電視信號。

drink

飲料：喝

drink to something
(happiness/good health)
為（幸福／健康）乾杯

drink up
很快喝完

cold **drink**
冷飲

fizzy **drink**
起泡沫的飲料，比如可樂等

hot **drink**
熱飲

soft **drink**
不含酒精的飲料

drinkable
可以飲用的

un**drink**able
不能飲用的

Do you prefer fizzy or still mineral water?
你想要可樂還是礦泉水？

Word Group

swallow
吞下

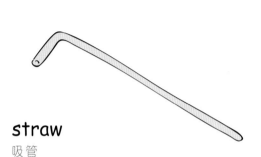

straw
吸管

liquid
液體

mineral water
礦泉水

sip
呷

squash
果汁飲料

suck
吸吮

swig
大口地喝

Drink up or we'll miss the start of the film.
快點喝完,不然我們就看不到電影的開頭了!

75

fresh food...
新鮮的食物

fresh air
（室外的）新鮮空氣

freshwater
淡水

fresh-faced
氣色好的；樣子年輕健康的

as **fresh** as a daisy
精神飽滿

convenience **food**
方便食品（只需加熱便可）

dog **food**
狗糧

frozen **food**
冷凍食物

sea**food**
海鮮

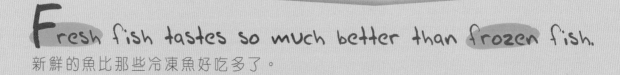

Fresh fish tastes so much better than frozen fish.
新鮮的魚比那些冷凍魚好吃多了。

chilled
冷凍的

stale
不新鮮的

planting
種植

aroma
香味

go off
食物變質；不喜歡；離開

market
市場

natural
天然的

preserved
用鹽醃製的；保鮮的

The aroma of fresh bread always makes me feel hungry.
新鮮麵包的香味總是讓我食指大動。

cook
廚師；烹調

cook up (an excuse)
編造（藉口）

cooked meat
煮熟了的肉

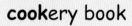

cooker
烹調用具

cookery book
烹飪書；食譜

cookery class
烹飪班

cooking oil
食用油

over**cook**ed
煮得過熟的

un**cook**ed
生的；未烹調的

This meat hasn't been cooked thoroughly.
肉還沒有完全煮透。

grill
燒烤

boil
煮沸；用水烹煮

burnt
燒焦的

chef
（酒店；餐廳）大廚

food order
點菜；訂菜

kitchen
廚房

restaurant
餐廳

raw
生的

Daniel is a brilliant cook but he is very messy in the kitchen!
丹尼烹調很有一手，但是每次都會把廚房弄得一團糟！

service

服務；招待

church service
教堂禮拜儀式

dinner service
完整一套的餐具

fire service
消防署

in/out of service
正在使用 / 已停用

room service
送酒菜到客房的服務

self-service restaurant
自助餐廳

service a car
維修和保養汽車

service station
（汽車）加油站

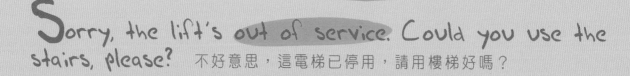

Sorry, the lift's out of service. Could you use the stairs, please? 不好意思，這電梯已停用，請用樓梯好嗎？

(fire/police) officer
官員（消防員；警察）

ceremony
典禮；儀式

food order
點菜；訂菜

break down
故障

customer
顧客

double fault
（網球）雙錯誤

guest
客人；嘉賓

waiter
侍應生

We stopped at the service station to fill up with petrol.
我們在加油站停下，給汽車加油。

tip
小費：提示

give someone a tip
給某人小費

No Tipping
禁止傾倒垃圾（告示）

on the tip of my tongue
話在嘴邊（卻一時想不起來）

tip of the iceberg
冰山一角

rubbish tip
垃圾堆；垃圾場

tip back
搖晃椅

tip-top
極好的

tiptoe
腳尖

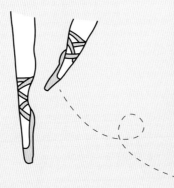

Helen's got to tidy her bedroom because it's a complete tip. 海倫的房間實在太亂了，她要好好收拾一下。

small change

零錢；找頭

iceberg

冰山；浮在海洋上的巨大冰塊

advice

忠告

bill

帳單

end

末端

point

尖端

pour

倒

dumper truck

自卸卡車

Ballet dancers learn to stand on the tips of their toes.

芭蕾舞蹈員正學習用腳尖站立。

Thursday

I went on holiday with my family. We were staying in a really nice hotel. My Mum was tired when we arrived so she phoned room service and ordered some sandwiches. In the evening, Mum and Dad wanted to eat in the hotel. There were lots of different restaurants serving Chinese, Western, Indian and fast food. My Dad wanted to eat Western food. He reserved a table by the window. We sat down and the waiter brought us the *menu*. It all looked horrible. There was no fast food such as burgers or chips. The only thing I could order was *salad*. I covered it in salad cream but it still tasted yukky.

I'm going to choose the restaurant next time!

I went to visit Uncle John. He owns a restaurant near where we live. He took me into the kitchen. The head _chef_ was wearing a big white hat and all the kitchen staff were wearing white jackets. They looked really cool even though it got very hot when all the ovens were on! The waiters were rushing in and out carrying the food orders. I really enjoyed watching the _chefs_ prepare the food. They use lots of herbs and spices when they're cooking. One of the chefs put a lot of meat under the _grill_ and asked me to make sure it didn't get burnt. I want to work in a restaurant when I leave school.

85

Series Name ： A Voyage in Everyday Words
Book Name ： A Voyage in Everyday Words: SHOPPING AND ENTERTAINMENT
Authors ： Jeremy and Sara Walenn
Editor ： Leung Ho Yan
Published by ： The Commercial Press (H.K.) Ltd.
8/F, Eastern Central Plaza, 3 Yiu Hing Road, Shau Kei Wan, Hong Kong
http://www.commercialpress.com.hk
Distributed by ： SUP Publishing Logistics (HK) Limited
3/F, C & C Building, 36 Ting Lai Road, Tai Po, N.T., Hong Kong
Printed by ： C & C Offset Printing Co., Ltd.
C & C Building, 36 Ting Lai Road, Tai Po, N.T., Hong Kong
Edition ： First Edition, October 2010
© 2010 The Commercial Press (Hong Kong) Ltd.
ISBN 978 962 07 1921 9
Printed in Hong Kong

系列名：A Voyage in Everyday Words

書名：A Voyage in Everyday Words: SHOPPING AND ENTERTAINMENT

作者：Jeremy and Sara Walenn

責任編輯：梁可茵

出版：商務印書館 (香港) 有限公司

香港筲箕灣耀興道3號東滙廣場8樓

http://www.commercialpress.com.hk

發行：香港聯合書刊物流有限公司

香港新界大埔汀麗路36號中華商務印刷大廈3字樓

印刷：中華商務彩色印刷有限公司

香港新界大埔汀麗路36號中華商務印刷大廈

版次：2010年10月第1次印刷